GRACIE, La Roo

SETS SAIL

written by MARSHA QUALEY

illustrated by KRISTYNA LITTEN

PICTURE WINDOW BOOKS
a capstone imprint

Gracie LaRoo Sets Sail is published by
Picture Window Books, a Capstone imprint
1710 Roe Crest Drive
North Mankato, MN 56003
www.mycapstone.com

Library of Congress Cataloging-in-Publication data is
available on the Library of Congress website.

Summary: Gracie saves the day when she teams up
with some tap-dancing sows on a cruise ship, making
the Water Sprites' performance spectacular!

ISBN 978-1-5158-1439-9 (library binding)
ISBN 978-1-5158-1443-6 (ebook pdf)

Designer: Aruna Rangarajan

Editor: Megan Atwood

Production Specialist: Steve Walker

Printed and bound in the USA
010401F17

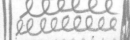

TABLE OF CONTENTS

GRACIE and The

NAME: Gracie LaRoo

TEAM: Water Sprites

CLAIM TO FAME:
Being the youngest pig
to join a world-renowned
synchronized swimming team!

SIGNATURE MOVE:
"When Pigs Fly" Spin

LIKES: Purple, clip-on tail bows,
mud baths, new-mown hay
smell

DISLIKES: Too much attention,
doing laundry, scary movies

QUOTE

"I just hope I can be the kind of synchronized
swimmer my team needs!"

WATER SPRITES

JINI

BARB

JIA

SU

MARTHA

BRADY

SILVIA

A STERN CAPTAIN

Gracie LaRoo stood at the rail of the ship and watched dolphins frolic in the ocean.

"Welcome aboard, cousin," a voice called.

Gracie spun around. "Joanna! It's so great to see you! And this cruise ship is just beautiful. Thank you so much for inviting us!"

The two cousins hugged. Then Joanna asked, "Where are the Water Sprites?"

"Still sleeping," Gracie said. "Everyone got to bed late because they were so excited. I am, too!" Then Gracie wrung her hooves. "At first the Sprites weren't sure performing on this cruise was a good idea. But I convinced them we would get new fans if we did shows here!"

Suddenly Joanna's eyes got
wide and she straightened up.

Gracie said, "What's wrong?"

But Joanna spoke to someone
behind Gracie. "Hello, Captain,"
she said.

Gracie turned around.

A sow in a splendid uniform
walked up to them. She said to
Joanna, "This must be one of the
swimmers." Her voice sounded
stern.

Joanna nodded, and the captain continued. She looked at Gracie. "Your team has won many medals. I hope you can put on a good show. Joanna says you can. I'm putting my trust in her."

With that, the captain walked away.

Joanna turned to Gracie with wide, nervous eyes. Gracie hugged her and said, "We will make you proud! We can't wait to perform!"

DISASTER!

Joanna showed Gracie around
the ship. When they reached the
top deck she said, "This is where
the Sprites will perform every
afternoon."

Gracie was delighted. A water slide towered above the glittering pool.

Suddenly Joanna shouted, "Stop, ma'am. The pool is not open yet!"

A sow in an orange robe was dipping a hoof in the water. She said,

"The captain told me I could have a quick dip before I taught my first class. I am Rita Sinclair."

Gracie whispered, "You didn't tell me there was a famous dancer on the ship!"

Joanna nodded excitedly. Then she said to the sow, "Miss Sinclair, I didn't recognize you. I am so sorry."

Miss Sinclair smiled and said, "Quite all right, sweetie!" Then she dropped her robe and dove into the water.

That afternoon the Sprites got ready for their first show on the ship.

The dressing room was busy
and loud.

Joanna poked her head in the
door. "We're ready at the pool,"
she said. "The captain is there."

Her eyes got wide and Gracie

winked at her to reassure her.

As the team lined up for their

entrance walk, Gracie wished:

Please, please, please let it all be perfect!

But everything was not perfect.

Tiny piglets ran around their

legs as they entered.

Pigs booed and shouted as the

Sprites performed.

One piglet threw a beach ball

at the Wiggly Piggly Pyramid. The

Sprites fell and broke apart, belly-

flopping into the pool.

After that, piglets thought it was funny to throw all sorts of things at the Sprites.

Gracie's triple spin was a triple tumble into the water.

When she popped back up, she saw the Captain near Joanna at the side of the pool.

The captain was frowning and shaking her head.

CHAPTER 3

GRACIE'S IDEA

Joanna joined the team at dinner. "I am so sorry about the show."

Barb said, "That crowd was wild and mad. They wanted to be in the pool."

Joanna said, "The captain got many complaints about the pool and water slide being closed."

She looked near tears. "She's afraid we might have to . . . cancel all your performances!"

All the Sprites gasped.

"I persuaded the captain to let you have one more chance," Joanna said. "But she told me that if you don't make the crowd happy, then you will get off the ship at Port Wallow and go home."

"Oh, no!" said Su. "What if the news gets out that the Water Sprites failed?"

"We wanted new fans," added Martha. "Not enemies."

Gracie didn't want her friends to see her tears. She said, "I'm going for a walk."

Disaster! she thought, as she hurried away. How could she fix it?

As Gracie walked on an upper deck, thinking hard, she heard music and thumping from one of the activity rooms.

Tap dancing!

Gracie peeked into the room.

It was crowded with older

sows. At the very front, with her

back to the room, danced Rita

Sinclair.

Gracie watched and listened as the famous dancer called out steps, and the other dancers followed along. Miss Sinclair led the dancers around the room in a long line.

Gracie smiled. She had a perfect idea.

A FABULOUS SHOW

When the class was over, Gracie slipped inside.

Miss Sinclair was talking with three of the dancers.

One of the dancers noticed Gracie, "You're one of the swimming pigs! I saw your show yesterday."

Another dancer said, "Those piglets were terrible, the way they threw things at you."

Miss Sinclair wrinkled her snout. "Piglets bothered a performer? Unacceptable!"

The third dancer said, "If my grandpigs did something like that they would be in trouble."

Gracie said, "Miss Sinclair, you don't know me but I'm a big fan. I've watched videos of your Hogway shows over and over."

"How very sweet," said Miss Sinclair, curtseying.

"And when I was watching the class," Gracie continued, "I had an idea how to make our next show go better. But I would need your help." She looked at the other dancers. "In fact, we would need all of you to help us."

The next afternoon a huge crowd waited by the pool.

"There are so many people today," Jini said to Gracie.

"Rita and her dancers certainly spread the word!" said Gracie.

When the music began, Miss Sinclair led two lines of tap-dancing sows through the crowd to the pool. At the water's edge, the lines danced apart.

There were the Water Sprites!

The dancers tapped into position all around the pool, and the Sprites dove in.

With Miss Sinclair and the
grannies on guard, no piglets
caused trouble.

With Miss Sinclair and the
grannies leading the cheers,
the crowd joined in.

The show was like a wonderful dream.

The Dolphin Arches Formation made a beautiful circle.

The Wiggly Piggly Pyramid rose high above the water.

Gracie's final spin into the pool dazzled the crowd.

When she burst back up, she heard a fresh roar of applause.

She saw piglets dancing with the sows. She saw smiling faces.

And she saw the captain hugging Joanna. She heard the captain say, "What a great idea, Joanna! How many shows can we get them to do?"

Gracie twirled happily.

GLOSSARY

belly-flop — to land on your stomach

curtsey — to put one foot in front of the other and to bend the knees as a way of formally greeting someone; normally done by women or girls

dazzling — exciting!

frolic — to run around and play

glittering — sparkling

persuade — to talk someone into something

splendid — beautiful and lovely

TALK ABOUT IT!

1. Piglets on the ship were very rowdy. Have you been in a situation when kids around you were being rowdy? What did you do?

2. Why do you think the piglets calmed down when the grannies stepped in?

3. Gracie was afraid she'd put her teammates in a bad situation. Have you ever felt that way? Were you able to make the situation better?

WRITE ABOUT IT!

1. Pretend you are Gracie's cousin, Joanna. Write a letter to the captain of the ship asking if the Water Sprites could perform.

2. Write a letter from Gracie to Rita, thanking her for helping out the Water Sprites.

3. Write a story from the point of view of one of the piglets on the ship. What was it like to see the Water Sprites perform?

About the Author

Marsha Qualey is the author of many books for readers young and old. Though she learned to swim when she was very young, she says she has never tried any of the moves and spins Gracie does so well.

Marsha has four grown-up children and two grandchildren. She lives in Wisconsin with her husband and their two non-swimming cats.

About the Illustrator

Kristyna Litten is an award winning children's book illustrator and author. After studying illustration at Edinburgh College of Art, she now lives and works from Yorkshire in the UK, with her pet rabbit Herschel.

Kristyna would not consider herself a very good swimmer as she can only do the breaststroke, but when she was younger, she would do a tumble roll and a handstand in the shallow end of the pool.

THE WONDERFUL, THE AMAZING, THE PIG-TASTIC GRACIE LAROO!

Discover more at
www.capstonekids.com

- Find out more about Gracie and her adventures.
- Follow the Water Sprites as they craft their routines.
- Figure out what you would do . . . if you were the awesome Gracie LaRoo!